To my beloved John, the man who
shares the front seat with me
—I.O.G.

For Mum, with gratitude and big love
—C.J.

The Scrubbly-Bubbly Car Wash
Text copyright © 2003 by Irene O'Garden   Illustrations copyright © 2003 by Cynthia Jabar
Manufactured in China. All rights reserved.   www.harperchildrens.com Library of Congress Cataloging-in-Publication Data
O'Garden, Irene.   The scrubbly-bubbly car wash / by Irene O'Garden ; pictures by Cynthia Jabar.   p.   cm.
Summary: Rhythmic, rhyming text describes what happens as a car goes through a car wash.
ISBN 0-694-00871-0 — ISBN 0-06-029486-8 (lib. bdg.)
[1. Car washes—Fiction.   2. Stories in rhyme.]   I. Jabar, Cynthia, ill.
II. Title.   PZ8.3.O245 Sc   2001   [E]—dc21   00-032022
Typography by Elynn Cohen 1 2 3 4 5 6 7 8 9 10 ✤ First Edition

The Scrubbly-Bubbly Car Wash

by Irene O'Garden

illustrated by Cynthia Jabar

HarperCollins*Publishers*

What do we get for driving far?

A crusty, dusty, dirty car.

How are we to get it clean?

I know just where to go, by gosh!
To the scrubbly-bubbly CAR WASH!

We pay the man and he smiles back.
Our windows are up, we're on the track.

We hear a funny whumping sound
as floods of suds come foaming down
at the lathery-blathery,
scrubbly-bubbly CAR WASH!

Soapy floppy brushes mop
from our tires to our top.

Steamy sprays beyond the brushes
rinse us down in luscious rushes

at the drippity-droppity, bottom-to-toppity, lathery-blathery, scrubbly-bubbly CAR WASH!

The dryer goes on with a thundery sound.
Water drops stretch and race around.

We cross a carousel of cloth
that pats our car and dries it off
in that clickety-clackety, rattley-rackety,
drippity-droppity, bottom-to-toppity,
lathery-blathery, scrubbly-bubbly CAR WASH!

And out of the soapy thunderstorm
we drive, still safe and dry and warm,

all mopped and sponged and swabbed and clean,

thanks to the magical machine . . .

of the sparkly-shimmery, glittery-glimmery,
clickety-clackety, rattley-rackety,
drippity-droppity, bottom-to-toppity,
lathery-blathery, scrubbly-bubbly CAR WASH!